Show Off

Story by Carmel Reilly

Illustrations by Pat Reynolds

Contents

Chapter 1
At the Stadium

"Wow," said Eddie as he arrived for his first training session with the Junior Super Stars. "This place is enormous!"

Brad Hill, Eddie's new coach, grinned. "We have five courts here at the stadium," he said, "so there's lots of room for all our teams to practise."

Eddie stood with his dad and his friend, Nina, and waited for the other players to arrive.

Nina nudged Eddie. "Look," she said. "There's that boy Dylan we met at the park a while ago. He must be in the team, too."

Eddie turned around and watched Dylan and his dad as they walked over to talk to Brad Hill. He remembered that Dylan's dad used to play for the City Super Stars when he was younger.

"It's not going to be much fun playing with Dylan," groaned Eddie. "He's an amazing player, but he is such a show off."

"Brad wouldn't have chosen him if he didn't think he could fit into the team," Eddie's dad reassured him.

"I hope so," said Nina.

Chapter 2

Choosing the Team

Brad Hill called the players over.

"Welcome to the Junior Super Stars, everyone," he said. "Today I need to choose the main players for the team this Saturday. We'll have a practice game now so I can see how you all work together."

Brad put the children into two teams. "You five are on one side," he said, "and you five are on the other side."

Eddie's heart sank when he saw that he was going to be on the same side as Dylan.

The game started, and one of the girls threw the ball to Eddie. But Dylan swooped between them and grabbed it.

He ran quickly, dribbled the ball to the other end and scored. He yelled loudly and punched the air.

A little later, Eddie had the ball and was dribbling it to the end of the court. But before he could aim at the basket, Dylan snatched the ball from him and took a shot. He whooped and yelled as the ball flew through the ring.

After a few minutes, Brad blew his whistle. "Let's take a break," he said.

Nina ran over to talk to Eddie. "I can't believe what Dylan's doing. He grabs the ball all the time, even when he doesn't need to," she said.

"I know," said Eddie. "It's really annoying. And Brad will probably think Dylan's better than everyone else because he's always in the middle of the play."

11

At the end of practice, Brad called everyone over. He was just about to tell them who would be the main players on Saturday, when Dylan called out.

"Brad! What position will I have?" he asked.

Brad frowned. "You're a good player, Dylan," he said. "But you need to work more with the others before you are ready to play in the main team. This Saturday, I want you to be a substitute."

Dylan looked shocked.

"Now, for this week, I'd like to see these people on the court," said Brad, calling out five names. Eddie leapt up when he heard he was one of them.

Chapter 3

The Game

Eddie arrived at the stadium early on Saturday morning. He was surprised to see Dylan already waiting. Eddie walked over to him.

"Are you all right?" he asked.

"I wish I was playing today," said Dylan glumly. "At practice, I was trying so hard to impress everyone that I forgot about teamwork."

"Your dad was a great team player," said Eddie.

"I know," said Dylan. "I wish I could show him today that I really can play well in a team."

A few minutes into the game, the centre player, Bella, tripped and fell. The players gathered around as Brad helped her back to the bench.

"We need someone to take Bella's place," said Brad. He looked at the players on the bench. For a moment, he looked straight at Dylan, but then he moved on.

"Harry, can you go on now?" he asked.

At half-time, the team was down by eight points and some of the children were starting to look tired.

Dylan put his hand up. "Please, can I go on for a while?" he asked. "I could give someone a rest."

"I know he'll play well," said Eddie.

Brad looked hard at Dylan. "All right, Dylan, you can give Mara a break," he said, finally.

Dylan took a deep breath and ran onto the court.

Chapter 4

Team Players

Eddie chased the other team's centre player as he dribbled the ball down the court. The centre passed the ball to another player, but Eddie zipped across in front of him and snatched it.

To his left, Eddie could see Dylan waving his arms. Eddie quickly flipped the ball up and over the heads of the other team. Dylan jumped up, grabbed the ball and ran.

Moments later, he had scored.

Eddie raced back to defend at the other end. As the ball rebounded from the backboard, he leapt high to catch it.

Soon the ball was back down to Dylan. He aimed at the basket.

But, as Eddie appeared, Dylan quickly passed the ball to him. Eddie scored again.

Dylan gave Eddie a high five. "That was great," he said.

"I couldn't have done it without you," Eddie replied.

At the end of the game, Brad spoke to the team.

"I was very happy with the way you all played today, especially Eddie and Dylan," he said.

Dylan and Eddie grinned at each other.

"I think you both got to show off your talents in the best possible way," Brad added, "as team players."